Werner Mittelstaedt
Wolf Heidecker

Tipping Point 2029

A Play on Climate Change

Bibliografische Informationen der Deutschen Nationalbibliothek:
Die Deutsche Nationalbibliothek verzeichnet diese Publikation in der Deutschen Nationalbibliografie; detaillierte bibliografische Daten sind im Internet über http://dnb.d-nb.de abrufbar.

Tipping Point 2029
A Play on Climate Change

Werner Mittelstaedt und Wolf Heidecker

Redaktionelle Mitarbeit und Lektorat:
Mechthild Mittelstaedt, Haltern am See

Umschlagabbildung: © boscorelli/Shotshop.com

© 2022 Werner Mittelstaedt, Haltern am See und
Wolf Heidecker, Werribee Vic 3030, Australia

Herstellung und Verlag:

BoD – Books on Demand, Norderstedt

ISBN 978-3-7543-4396-8

Content

Characters
In alphabetical order

Julian **Berndes**, CEO of ABC-TV (age 45-55, casual dress, no tie)

Steven **Fissler**, Sociologist, Futurologist (age 50-65, professional, casual)

Walter **Millert**, CEO of an Energypower Group (age 55-65, formal attire)

Joseph **Molden**, Federal Minister for Infrastructure, Transport, Regional Development and Communication (age 55-60, formal attire)

Frank **Rauter**, Movie/Theatre Director, Author and Action-Artist (age 30-45, casual)

Bettina **Roland**, TV-Presenter (age 40-50, professional, elegant attire)

Mia **Schellinger**, Eco-Activist with »Degrowth-Movement« (age 27, eco dress)

Paula **Spiteri**, Evolutionary Biologist, Ecologist (age 40-50, professional, elegant attire)

First scene

When the curtain rises, the elegantly dressed presenter Bettina Roland stands alone in the studio. She wants to get in the mood a little for the moderation of the recording of live discussion that is about to begin. She is still stressed from the preparations for her show.

PRODUCER

One hour to the start of the recording of the panel discussion. 60 minutes call!

BETTINA ROLAND

The final editorial review was far too long. *(checks her Smartwatch)* Blood pressure too high, pulse too high, blood sugar levels not optimal, wet hands, not done enough physical work today, possible weak concentration during the show. *(She takes off her shoes and jacket, which she places over one of the seven chairs and does a few loosening exercises. Then she wipes herself dry with a handkerchief and takes a glass of mineral water that is on the table. She puts her shoes and jacket back on and sits down quite casually on one of the seven chairs, looking slightly exhausted.)*

The team should not turn up for another 15 minutes. *(just about getting a cigarette out of the package the producer walks in)*

PRODUCER

Everything okay?

BETTINA ROLAND

My introduction is OK. The only people I have to be really wary of are the sometimes rather unpredictable action artist and the fairly freaked-out activist of the Degrowth-Movement who as far as I know can be rather dogmatic. *(mockingly – imitating the CEO Julian Berndes)*

The discussion is not meant to unsettle the audience at all; it is meant to make them confident about the near future. So, I just shouldn't let them talk too much. The other guests are, in my estimation, easy. I've had the slick Millert and the self-righteous Federal Minister Molden several times in past shows. I find them both extraordinarily lousy, but they are really well suited for this discussion.

PRODUCER

You are aware that this discussion will reach the biggest audience you have ever had. It will be broadcast throughout our entire network and shown with subtitles in more than 20 countries. That's a new one – another Australian first! *(leaves the studio)*

BETTINA ROLAND *(mobile phone rings)*

Hello Darling, yes, I am fine, and how are you, Ben? The recording of the show starts soon, so unfortunately, we haven't got much time. Yes, Ben, I will host the show calmly.

I've been doing it for almost ten years and I've never let my guests throw me. I guess I'll be home around eleven, eleven-thirty. Please turn down the air conditioning in the bedroom as it may be getting quite hot later. It hasn't been quite so hot outside for a few days now, after all. With thirty-nine degrees during the day and a bit over thirty degrees at night, we both manage well. Besides, we still have our trusty Turbo-air con.

Yes, I've just said that. I don't know, anyway, you can do pretty much anything else with me. ... Oh, I would like that too. I love you too. (*Molden and Millert cross the rear of the studio*)

Hold on, there are already guests straying around in the studio. We have to end this conversation right now. See you later, darling. Bye.

Welcome Minister, nice to see you again; hello Mr Millert, you too of course. Please proceed to the Guest Lounge, Alan, our producer will look after you.

(*after they leave Bettina lights a cigarette and moves to the opposite corner of the studio – Julian Berndes walks in*)

JULIAN BERNDES

Good evening, Bettina!

BETTINA ROLAND

(*tries to hide the cigarette*)
Oh, Julian, good evening. What a surprise. What is the almighty CEO doing in my humble abode? I actually want to get in the mood for the show and need some peace and time to concentrate.

JULIAN BERNDES

I came because you smoked.

BETTINA ROLAND

How do you know I've been smoking here? You don't seriously come into the studio to check whether I smoke here. This isn't kindergarten.

JULIAN BERNDES

No, I was just joking. Actually, as you surely know smoking has been completely banned in public places since January 2025, meaning here as everywhere else in Australia. The fines are really high. But, (mockingly) dear Ms Roland, the whole team knows that you are smoking at least one cigarette in the studio

before every show. Even I have known it for a very long time…
and I'm okay with it.

BETTINA ROLAND

No way…?!

JULIAN BERNDES

Yes, but please don't tell the team. Because I promised never to
tell.

BETTINA ROLAND

It's all right. It's a really good team, isn't it?

JULIAN BERNDES

Yes, a really good team. Well, in about 45 minutes the discussion will start. I just want to tell you something or give you some
advice.

BETTINA ROLAND

Now, let's be clear. What's up?

JULIAN BERNDES

Especially with today's show we and the entire network are bearing a great responsibility. You must have a clear understanding about the aim of the discussion.

BETTINA ROLAND

Sorry, that's not good enough to talk to me like this so close to the show. All the important issues have been addressed and discussed in the editorial meeting we just had. The concept of this show is in place and keep in mind I will protect my independence and journalistic freedoms, that's how I do my job and it certainly wouldn't be so successful if it hasn't been like this for many years now. Therefore, you should know that you - actually - can't give me any instructions how to conduct my shows, even though you are the CEO. I don't let anyone tell me how to manage my show. For today I got all the editorial help and the necessary background knowledge required, as always. For this show, the goal was discussed with me in detail and I agree with it one hundred per cent. So, what is your problem?

JULIAN BERNDES

Before we continue, Bettina, can I have a ciggy too? Unfortunately, I haven't got mine with me. (*Bettina's rings. She accepts the call and moves away from Berndes*).

BETTINA ROLAND

Just a moment Julian, it's my mom. Hi Mum. How are you going with the heat today? (pause, as mother speaks). Oh, good, you really worried me the other day. (a bit impatient) My show is about to be recorded. (pause, mother speaks) I told you this morning! (pause) Oh, thank you, I'm sure it will go well too. Please drink lots of mineral water and keep as cool as possible. See you Monday, and say hi to Dad for me. Tell him to drink as much water as possible too. (pause, mother speaks) It's very important mum, you will dehydrate! I got to go now, bye Mum!
(*to Julian*) Here you go, your cigarette!

JULIAN BERNDES

Ta!

BETTINA ROLAND

You have surely heard that many years ago, during an interview with the late Brian Henderson, a colleague I always admired, Bob Hawke smoked one cigar after another with a can of beer in the other hand. That must have been about forty years ago. Today that would be utterly unfathomable. In 1990/91 smoking was banned from Parliament House, including all the PM's offices; violation of the policy became a punishable offence.

JULIAN BERNDES

Of course, I remember this interview. I'm pretty sure it was part of a documentary in 2006. He had smoked four cigars during the show. Eventually, Henderson offered Hawk a cigarette after he ran out of cigars. Then they both smoked in front of the camera. That was almost ridiculous back then and only possible because of Hawke.

Oh, that feels good. It's only my third today. Well, the air-conditioning systems are much better than they were back then, no smoke, no odour and even 99% of viruses, since Covid, are filtered out. The air quality here is certainly better than out there in the city and close to that you get in Tassie at a cool night.

BETTINA ROLAND

How do you know all that stuff about the air conditioners?

JULIAN BERNDES

I was recently invited to a product presentation by a company in Sydney that produces security technology and air-conditioning systems for television studios. It was very interesting.

BETTINA ROLAND

But now it's time. What exactly do you want to tell me and what is the ›advice‹? I am well aware of my responsibilities, so, let me hear your words of wisdom.

JULIAN BERNDES

That's right, I've never talked to you so close to start of a show. But this is a really special one. It's only been six days since the Intergovernmental Panel on Climate Change broke the terrible news of the »Tipping Point«. Ever since, there have already been a huge number of broadcasts on the subject worldwide - probably more than on any other event in recent decades. Your show should, indeed must, prevent a »second Spain«! Do you understand?

BETTINA ROLAND

By »second Spain« you surely refer to the talk show of colleague Miguel Ruiz on Wednesday on La1 and what happened in the aftermath?

JULIAN BERNDES

Of course. After this broadcast, there were major riots in some Spanish cities, but also in other places in Europe, Asia and America. The show made many people lose faith that something can still be done about the »Tipping Point« in order to noticeably and permanently improve the general quality of life. Critical intellectuals are talking about »a world without a future«. We have to avoid that to be repeated. The show on La 1 must have been the last straw for many people. I didn't think it was possible that television was still capable of mobilising so many people. But I wasn't the only one who was surprised.

BETTINA ROLAND

Of course, I also saw that live-stream. That's part of my job. Having been live-streamed in the net was why word quickly got around everywhere that the top-class scientists in this show, including three of the world's most renowned climate researchers, emphasised in unison that global warming will not be stopped, let alone turned around by 2050 but most probably continue to increase and lead to even worse consequences. They said that the global climate system has now finally tipped over as a result of decades of failure to take climate protection measures, which since Monday has been called the »Tipping Point«.

But, as I see it, the panel discussion was not very constructive as there were no answers or even the attempt to find answers as to how the future should now be shaped with the very high temperatures from spring to autumn, the strangely cold winters and all the other extreme weather events in order to even come close to regaining the general quality of life of years past. You see, I have done my homework.

JULIAN BERNDES

Well done! I know that you are good, very good, indeed the best. That's one of the reasons why I strongly lobbied for the renewal of your contract last year, and the increase of your contract.

BETTINA ROLAND

Thank you. But I think that my colleague Miguel Ruiz from La 1 nevertheless presented his programme very well. I was just thinking about the fact that my show should not promote resignation but hope. But I don't want to and can't tell my guests what they should say. I'm not censoring anything!

Oh, now we should finally get rid of the smoke. (*Both try to clear the cigarette mist from the studio. Berndes takes off his jacket and waves it in the air. In the process he loses his balance and falls down.*)

JULIAN BERNDES

Ow, that hurt. I lost my balance. Can't sleep properly for weeks because of the heat; I am so tired. Tell me - how do you deal with the heat? You always seem so fresh.

BETTINA ROLAND

Want a hand? Have you hurt yourself? Shall I call our first-aider? Do you need a doctor?

JULIAN BERNDES

No, thanks, I'm fine. I just need to drink some GETME-RIGHT.

BETTINA ROLAND

My God, you gave me a fright. I'm sorry you fell. Of course, I'm often exhausted too. So, I shower more often and drink a lot of mineral-water. Despite the heat, I try to be physically active as much as possible. I have had my trusty smartwatch for more than a year now, which almost completely monitors my health and gives me very good tips on how to maintain my health and fitness at a reasonably good level. It also tells me when I should see a doctor and what medicines and supplements I should take.

JULIAN BERNDES

But you are aware that any interested party out there who has the means could access your health data over the net?

BETTINA ROLAND

Yes, but I'm happy to put up with that.

JULIAN BERNDES

So, I am good again. Returning to your last comment. Of course you should not tell them what to say, we are not in China or Russia. But you should steer the discussion in the direction of encouraging your guests to focus on the fact that they are loo-king for ways out of the climate crisis and motivate the audience accordingly. You could emphasise that many scientists are constantly looking for solutions and perhaps suggest that they will certainly find some. If necessary, you should shorten or lengthen the panellists' speaking time. Have an eye on Mia Schellinger from the Degrowth-Movement and this »action-ar-tist« Rauter; we never had dealings with him before.

The aim of the show should be to contribute to a constructive debate for the whole of Australia in order to escape the tipping point trap. The »Tipping Point« should not be dramatized unne-cessarily in your show. Try to keep the ball flat.

BETTINA ROLAND

It's probably too late for that. If you wanted that, the show should have been planned differently and we should have in-vited different guests.

JULIAN BERNDES

That's true, unfortunately. But with the very short notice we got on Tuesday that the recording had to be rescheduled to today to allow the airing of your show the day after tomorrow in coordi-nation with the other five television stations, we could not have known at all that a program with comparable content would be broadcast on La 1 on Wednesday, with such fateful consequen-ces. (*Bettina Roland's smartwatch rings*)

BETTINA ROLAND

I would like to emphasise that having a »constructive debate« is ultimately not the responsibility of television, but of politics and social institutions. Strictly speaking, every individual is responsible for this. Everyone has to react somehow to the »Tipping Point«. Well, is what you are trying here coming from you or is there someone else behind it? (gesture upstairs)

JULIAN BERNDES

I just want this show not to further unsettle people and make them aggressive, as was done by the program in La 1.

BETTINA ROLAND

Of course, I don't want that either. But you didn't answer my question.

JULIAN BERNDES

That's all I can say.

BETTINA ROLAND

Thank you, you have actually answered my question. So, you got pressure from upstairs.

PRODUCER

Recording starts in 15 minutes.

BETTINA ROLAND

Please go now! Not much time left. I have to concentrate on the show now and have my make-up done. A cup of coffee would be nice. The panelists are already in the Green-Room, the audience enters the studio ten minutes before the recording.

JULIAN BERNDES

I wish you every success and hope that the discussion takes the desired course.

BETTINA ROLAND

I'm not quite sure about that. The atmosphere among the peop¬le is heated like the weather. My guests will certainly talk about that, too.

JULIAN BERNDES

I'm counting on you!

BETTINA ROLAND

I will do my best.

JULIAN BERNDES

Thank you, and good luck.

PRODUCER *(announcement to all)*

10 minutes to the official start of the recording. Please take your
seats.

(while panelists enter in the background - directly to the audience)

Second scene

Good afternoon, Ladies and Gentlemen, welcome to Studio 17. My name is Alan Spencer, acting producer of today's show.

Please let me remind you that with your ticket to the recording of today's episode of the Bettina Roland Show »Now and The Future« which will be aired the day after tomorrow you have accepted all terms and conditions.

When entering this studio our Cyber-Security System has scanned your personal communication devices and blocked them remotely from sending, receiving and recording. Once you leave the studio the functions will be reinstated automatically.

We have eight camera points in this studio covering the stage and the auditorium. If you are sitting next to someone you don't want the world to know about – just behave yourselves.

Cheers.

PAULA SPITERI

Good evening Ms Roland, good evening (waving hand to the other panelists who great each other)

BETTINA ROLAND

It's my pleasure to welcome the world-renowned sociologist and futurologist Steven Fissler. He wrote the world bestseller »The Climate Shock and the Future of Humanity« two years ago. This book has sold more than ten million copies and has been translated into twenty-eight languages. I would also like to add that Steven Fissler has written important socially critical books on the global crisis in recent decades, some of which have triggered heated debates. It's great that we were able to win you for this show Professor Fissler. For tonight you have agreed on taking on the difficult mission of explaining in plain English to our audiences what the »Tipping Point« means, in an easily comprehensible way.

(Bettina Roland looks at Mia Schellinger)

Now I welcome Mia Schellinger from country Victoria. She has been awarded the Alternative Nobel Prize 2028. Although she is just twenty-seven years old, she has received this important prize for her many achievements with the Degrowth-Movement. She has developed - and this has had a significant influence on the awarding of the prize - a contradiction-free system for right ways of living in theory and practice. Her system meets the strictest criteria of the sustainability principle. I am very pleased to have Mia Schellinger with us tonight; welcome!

MIA SCHELLINGER

Good evening Ms Roland, good evening. It was my pleasure to follow your invitation, however, having realized who the fellow panel members are I am feeling quite uncomfortable having to sit in the same room with Mr Millert and Mr Molden.

BETTINA ROLAND

Oh, I am surprised, Mia. You must have known that Walter Millert and the Federal Minister for Infrastructure, Transport, Regional Development and Communications, Joseph Molden, would be here today. They are very important discussion partners for this evening, same as you.

MIA SCHELLINGER

No, I didn't know that when I accepted on Wednesday. If I had known, I certainly would have prepared myself accordingly.

BETTINA ROLAND

But you have to accept all the guests tonight.

MIA SCHELLINGER

Well, now I have to, don't I?

BETTINA ROLAND

Now I welcome Walter Millert, CEO of Energypower Group Ltd based in Sydney. He has been working for this major energy company for more than two decades, fifteen years as a member of the board of directors, and for the past eight years as their CEO. Walter Millert will not be able to deny that the switch to renewable energy in the group he leads has been far too slow to date. After all, Energypower Group still generates most of its electricity from the highly climate-damaging fossil fuels Lignite, Coal and Gas. I am pleased you agreed to join this discussion panel where you can expect probably some quite uncomfortable questions of my other guests you knew would be here today.

WALTER MILLERT

Good evening Ms Roland. Mia Schellinger's comments are utterly beyond me; I can't wait to see what this discussion brings. I am not afraid to give very uncomfortable answers to uncomfortable questions.

BETTINA ROLAND

Now I would like to welcome Frank Rauter. As a director, action artist and book author you have been active on many levels for many years.

In recent years, he has sharply and repeatedly criticised the destruction of the biological foundations of our existence by global capitalism. He has also written and directed several plays to that avail. He is constantly using social media pointing out social and political grievances. A few months ago, together with Greenpeace, he carried out a spectacular action in the Antarctic to draw attention to the dramatic melting of the ice shelf »Larsen C« so that drastic measures for climate protection promised by governments for a long time would finally be realised. During this action, he lost two toes on his right foot. The toes had to be amputated. Glad you have recovered from this ordeal, Frank.

FRANK RAUTER

Thank you, Bettina, good evening everyone. Incidentally, I fully endorse what Mia said about Mr Millert and Mr Molden. Both are particularly to blame for the fact that the »Tipping Point« has now been reached. They do not belong in a show like this, but before a tribunal that condemns those primarily responsible for driving the world to the »Tipping Point«.

(Producer on high alert, ready to intervene if situation escalates)

MIA SCHELLINGER

Thank you Frank for your support. I am glad that you are here. Otherwise I would have left.

BETTINA ROLAND

Frank, I ask you to remain objective. This show is not intended to establish the guilt of individuals for the »Tipping Point«. Ultimately, we want to make constructive contributions to the future with this discussion.

FRANK RAUTER

But I found my observation quite constructive.

WALTER MILLERT

You, Mr Rauter, don't know what nonsense you have just put into the world. You should be ashamed of yourself!

FRANK RAUTER

But I don't!

JOSEPH MOLDEN

Mr Millert, ignore Rauter. It's not worth going into the bullshit he just said.

WALTER MILLERT

Thank you, I'll try.

BETTINA ROLAND

Well, can I move on now?! Last but not least, ladies and gentlemen, I welcome Joseph Molden. If this show would only be broadcast in Australia, I wouldn't need to introduce him, because according to a recent survey, more than ninety percent of all Ossies aged between eighteen and eighty know him. The Right Honorable Joseph Molden has been a member of parliament for thirty-five years. For three years now, he has held office as Federal Minister for Infrastructure, Transport, Regional Development and Communication in the coalition of the Liberals, Nationals and the Greens. I am very pleased that you are here.

JOSEPH MOLDEN

Thank you very much, Ms Roland. Good evening. I look forward to having a debate that remains objective and hope we are keeping to the facts. The polemics and absurd accusations we have just heard are completely unacceptable. (talking to the producer) Hope this pathetic episode will not be included in any way! We need calm discussions and good decisions to be able to master the future in view of the »Tipping Point«. That is what I am here for tonight.

PRODUCER

Okay – five minute call.

BETTINA ROLAND

So, ladies and gentlemen. Let me give you a short run-down as to how todays show is designed. (first mainly addressing panelists, then studio audience)

Let's start with recounting all the crisis and catastrophes that have arisen as a result of global warming which lead to the »Tipping Point«. Then we shall hear your respective expert opinions in view of options and opportunities to prevent the climate change from worsening, ideally how the problem could be partially or even completely resolved in the medium to long term.

I do hope, I actually expect that we will be able to convey a positive view on the future, that we point out perspectives that bring hope to the audience all over the world at the end of this show.

For those of you who are not familiar with this talk show, here some brief information: My shows are hosted differently than most talk shows around the world. I ask the first question to a guest. After that, my guests can ask further questions or discuss and comment on what has been brought up so far. Of course, I also ask further questions and will make sure that we stick to certain topics and that the time limits for each individual speaker are kept. There are neither commercial breaks nor supporting film clips in my talk show. However, as a special feature breaking news and facts related to the relevant topic will be interspersed in irregular intervals.

PRODUCER

30 seconds – getting serious now. Camera, Sound!

BETTINA ROLAND

(changed demeanor, aware of camera live)

My first question to Professor Steven Fissler. Please tell our audience in a few words what lead to what has now been called the »Tipping Point« and what that actually means.

STEVEN FISSLER

Well, the topic is, as you may appreciate, very complex and it is far too little time to go into much detail. That's why I can only provide a rough sketch here, which I try to keep as easily understandable as possible, avoiding certain technical terms or other academic jargon. As I expected to be asked this question that requires individual details to be extremely precise, not least because of the many millions of viewers who will be listening in, I took some notes to be on the safe side. (Steven Fissler takes his notes out of his jacket and reads.)

So, the ›Noughties‹ were significantly warmer than the 1990s and these were warmer than the 1980s.

The 2010s were once again warmer than the Noughties and the years since 2020 have again been warmer than the 2010s.

Since the start of regular weather recordings in Australia in 1880, there has been the warmest phase on Earth at least from the turn of the century. Except for 1998, all the warmest years are in the new century. Strictly speaking, serious global warming started with the beginning of the second industrial revolution in the late 19th century, because since then the average global temperature has been rising steadily, which has been observed especially since the 1970s.

There is a close correlation between the increase of CO_2 concentration in the atmosphere and global warming. Before the beginning of the industrialisation, the global CO_2 concentration in the atmosphere was only 280 parts per million air molecules. In 2000 it was already 368, in 2015 it was just over 400 parts per million air molecules, and today we are well above that.

The last few decades were therefore de facto the warmest in the history of climate documentation. In addition, the last few decades have been incessantly warmer, with some years being among the warmest ever recorded. The current warming phase on Earth is considerably faster than any other known in the last sixty-five million years.

It is interesting to note that the warming records of recent years have occurred despite the record weakness of the Sun, because for several decades now the Sun's luminosity has been at its lowest since satellite measurements began in the 1970s. But I must point out that decreasing solar activity, even if it were extreme, would make relatively little difference to manmade global warming. Probably, without decreasing solar activity, global warming would only be 0.1° to 0.3 ° Celsius higher by the end of this century.

FRANK RAUTER

Very important that you also address this aspect. Respect!
(Producer – goes to Bettina; gesture to tech to start recorded message.)

PRODUCER

Time for our first announcement.

VOICE OVER

Last year's heatwave killed over seventy thousand people in Europe. This was just announced by the World Health Organisation. This means that even more people died prematurely as a result of the almost annual European heat wave than in the year 2027. According to a just released bulletin from the Australian Department of Health last January an unusually high number of people died especially in Australia's South-East. The authorities hold a heatwave responsible with temperatures of more than 40°C for eight days and another 17 days with more than 30°C in a row which also lead to the Australian Open to be cut short. In Victoria alone more than 900 heat fatalities have been reported last January, about double the number of an average January. The most effected group of people were the elderly, those who lived on their own or patients with heart or lung problems.

BETTINA ROLAND

Professor Fissler, please continue.

STEVEN FISSLER

Thank you. (Steven Fissler reads from his notes again.)

With global warming, the temperature in the Arctic and parts of the Antarctic region have increased above average with fatal consequences. Due to the melting of their ice, sea levels are rising faster than expected. In addition, global warming is causing glaciers to recede worldwide.

Switzerland, for example, is expected to be largely glacier-free in thirty to fifty years, which unfortunately will also be the case for many other glacier areas on earth.

(Paula Spiteri - show of hands. Steven Fissler asks her to speak.)

PAULA SPITERI

I would like to add that the worldwide melting of glaciers will also jeopardize the drinking water supply for many millions of people. In addition, in some cases inland navigation on many rivers will become impossible. Furthermore, this will further accelerate the extinction of species in flora and fauna, which makes it even worse.

WALTER MILLERT

And winter tourism will probably suffer too.

MIA SCHELLINGER

That should be the least of our worries.

STEVEN FISSLER

I agree with your remarks. (Steven Fissler continues reading from his notes.)

So, the global community is facing unprecedented challenges. Well over a billion people live in or close to coastal areas, most of them in large cities. Nor should we forget the hundreds of millions of people who live along rivers. Their habitats are already under acute threat, as we all regularly hear in the news, if we are not already affected ourselves. It is highly likely that the sea level will rise by at least another sixty centimeters by the end of the century. Due to increasing global warming, it is sadly very likely that the sea level rise could also be much worse. If urgent actions are not taken immediately, epochal catastrophes are inevitable. Due to continuous global warming we already have to live with floods and inundations which will become even more frequent and severe, and in many countries either the periods of drought or the wet seasons are becoming longer and longer. It is highly likely that the number of extreme weather events with dramatic consequences for us humans, for flora and fauna and for infrastructures will continue to escalate.

MIA SCHELLINGER

But can you finally tell us why we reached the »Tipping Point« now?

PAULA SPITERI

(to Fissler) What you said was all important and very interesting. (to Schellinger) Let's not interrupt Professor Fissler and please let him finish his statement.

FRANK RAUTER

Mia, that's right. Let's hear out Professor Fissler.

STEVEN FISSLER

Thank you, before I can get into details, I've had to clarify some important background first. So, how did the »Tipping Point« occur now? We all know that the Earth's climate system is intrinsically complex. Most processes influence each other and thus determine the local and global climate. Wind systems, for example, are heavily dependent on air and water temperatures. Precipitation all over the world depends on this. The ice at the poles controls global climate to a not inconsiderable extent. If parts of these systems are altered by human influences, they may no longer function - they tilt, and irreversibly so. For this reason, they are called tipping elements or tipping points. The Intergovernmental Panel on Climate Change speaks of a »Tipping Point« in the singular. Meaning that the climate system on Earth in its entirety has tipped and that everything possible must be done to mitigate the associated effects. Well, we have just heard about the consequences that highlight the very fact.

BETTINA ROLAND

Thank you, my editorial team did a very good job. Professor, is the major or final tipping element that triggered the »Tipping Point« known to the Intergovernmental Panel on Climate Change? (Bettina Roland is handed a paper with a current news item by someone from the editorial team.)

PRODUCER

Sorry, another announcement.

STEVEN FISSLER

Well, go ahead.

**PRODUCER –
VOICE OVER**

The Federal Minister for Agriculture, Gladys Hancock, has just announced her resignation. The reasons she gave is the lack of political support on the states and municipal levels to work together on solving the drinking water crisis that has been going on for months. The actual drought has lasted for 13 months already, the longest period in 100 years. It's even worse than the drought of 2019 which was the driest and hottest year since official weather recordings in Australia.

BETTINA ROLAND

After this even more concerning news, I ask you, Professor Fissler, to continue.

STEVEN FISSLER

Thank you. Which tipping element finally triggered the global »Tipping Point« is certain. I have thoroughly examined all the detailed information provided by the World Climate Council. about the »Tipping Point«.

Please bear with me now as I have to make some more basic remarks first. The Potsdam Institute for Climate Impact Research names nine potential tipping elements about which there is no dissent among climate researchers worldwide. They are: the Arctic sea ice, the Greenland Ice Sheet, the West Antarctic

Ice Sheet, the boreal forests, also known as the taiga, the Amazon rainforest, the El Niño and the Southern Oscillation, the Sahara/Sahel and West African monsoon, the Indian summer monsoon and the thermohaline Atlantic circulation.

Describing them in detail cannot, of course, be done here due to time constraints. If the upper limit of even one of these tipping elements is exceeded, there is a high probability that another element in the global climate system will be affected. Some tipping elements can set in motion a self-accelerating climate change that would then be irreversible. That is exactly what has happened. I hardly like to say it because it's so bad, but the West Antarctic Ice Sheet has been proven to have tipped irreversibly. That means it will definitely disintegrate. It has also been proven that the melting of the Greenland Ice Sheet, which has been going on for decades, has a significant negative effect on the Indian summer monsoon. It has lost power because the ongoing melting of the Greenland Ice Sheet has already weakened and will continue to impair the Atlantic's overturning movement called the Atlantic Thermohaline Circulation. The West Antarctic Ice Sheet, which is in the process of dissolving, and the ongoing melting of the Greenland Ice Sheet will lead to a sea level rise of several metres in a few centuries and further accelerate global warming.

Thus, out of nine potential tipping elements in the global climate system, one has definitely tipped and two other tipping elements, the Indian Summer Monsoon and the Atlantic Thermohaline Circulation are already in the process of tipping.

They are weakening due to the melting of the Greenland Ice Sheet. This, too, is in danger of tipping or dissolving at some point. All of this created the »Tipping Point«! It's nothing but a vicious circle.

MIA SCHELLINGER

Oh, I see, the tipping elements are not linear – meaning if one of the tipping elements in the global climate system has reached its tipping point any effects on other tipping elements can't be mathematically predicted and may have unforeseeable consequences.

STEVEN FISSLER

Exactly. An example: Due to global warming, the ice floating on the sea surface in the North Polar region is melting. Since the surface of the water that is now directly exposed the sunlight is not reflected anymore but absorbed by the water, hence it is getting warmer.

An even faster melting of the ice in summer and the absence of new ice formation in winter are the consequences, which in turn can bring about major changes in the climate in other places, even far away ones, that we cannot precisely predict.

What is certain is that the global warming that led to the »Tipping Point« was triggered by the greenhouse gases we humans put into the atmosphere. Ninety-seven percent of all climate scientists are convinced of this because there is overwhelming evidence. In particular, CO2 and methane emissions should be mentioned here.

FRANK RAUTER

Too much CO2 in the atmosphere is like a soup that is too salty. If even a little too much salt were added to it, it would be inedible. 100 grams of soup must not contain more than about 0.3 grams to a maximum of 0.5 grams of salt. This maximum salt content applies to all foods. More salt in 100 grams of food, with a few exceptions, would make us very sick.

PAULA SPITERI

A great analogy, because the extra CO2 in the atmosphere is not only destroying but killing things. It destroys corals because the oceans are already over-acidified due to the absorption of too much CO2. Along with the corals, many other creatures in the oceans are also endangered. We should definitely take note of the fact that life on land is inextricably linked to the oceans. Marine protection is protection of life on land.

STEVEN FISSLER

There are climate models that are trying to depict global warming by the end of the 21st century under various conditions. As early as the 1990s, they considered developments similar to those we are experiencing today and predicted them quite correctly. They already assumed that global society was not doing enough to combat the additional greenhouse gases emitted into the atmosphere by us humans. These are the business-as-usual climate simulations.

Today, climate models have become even more accurate due to much more knowledge and the increased experience of climate researchers. In addition, we now have much faster supercomputers and more complex programming techniques. The current situation is absolutely worrying. But I would like to point out the following, especially since I will probably never have a larger more interested audience than today. The decimation and destruction of the Amazon rainforest area and other tropical rainforests by clearing for land has already had and still has serious adverse effects on global biodiversity and on river systems. The climatic »Tipping Point« would be reached when deforestation, smoke, sea surface temperature anomalies such as the El Niño phenomenon and global warming lead to a lack of precipitation in some regions. The absence of rainfall due to deforestation seems to become more frequent when the cleared areas exceed thirty percent. This must be prevented at all costs because it would undoubtedly contribute enormously to the rapid increase in global warming!

BETTINA ROLAND

If I understand you correctly, Professor Fissler, it is a proven fact that, ultimately the causes of the »Tipping Point« are human beings and in particular the greenhouse gases they emit into the world or into the atmosphere?

STEVEN FISSLER

Yes, without a doubt. This is a finding that practically every adult in the world should have internalised for well over thirty years. At the 1992 Earth Summit in Rio de Janeiro, climate change caused by human activities was recognised by the world community as a serious problem, but, with the exception of very few countries, has so far not been adequately actively addressed. In addition to the greenhouse gases emitted into the atmosphere there are unfortunately other factors that contribute to climate change. They, too, were and are caused by us humans. (Frank Rauter reports with a show of hands, Bettina Roland is handed a paper with a current message by someone from the editorial team at the same time.)

PRODUCER

A new announcement.:

VOICE OVER

Glacier mass loss again at record levels worldwide since the beginning of the 21. century. This is the worrying conclusion of a new study by the World Glacier Monitoring Service. For this study, some forty-seven thousand glaciers were observed, measured and meticulously analyzed.

BETTINA ROLAND

So, Frank, you wanted to say something.

FRANK RAUTER

Mr Fissler, what is your view on the possible problems with the permafrost in the north of Russia. The frozen ground there is slowly thawing due to global warming, too.

This activates bacteria that excrete methane gas. In addition, the thawing of the permafrost soils could also release huge amounts of CO2.

STEVEN FISSLER

That worries me a lot because huge areas are affected. Not only in Russia, but also in northern Canada, Alaska and Greenland. Moreover, methane is a much more effective greenhouse gas than CO2 but fortunately is staying in the atmosphere for a much shorter time than CO2. Incidentally, methane is also produced significantly by still increasing cattle farming and wet rice cultivation. In that sense, every beef steak we eat contributes, disproportionately relative to many other foods, to the man-made greenhouse effect.

Yes, the additional CO2 that can be released by the thawing is a ticking time bomb. If it were released in large quantities, it could significantly accelerate global warming as the amount of

CO2 trapped in the permafrost soils is gigantic. Some researchers estimate that it could be as much as nine hundred gigatons. That's more than we currently have in the entire atmosphere.

MIA SCHELLINGER

The majority of climate researchers stated the global temperature increase must be limited to well below 2.0° Celsius, if possible to a maximum of 1.5 ° Celsius compared to the pre-industrial value, in order to keep the extent of climate change within limits. This has been called for again and again by climate scientists at many UN climate conferences. Preparing for today's discussion I read again that especially at the Paris World Climate Conference of 2015, all one hundred and ninety-six countries on earth have agreed on the respective limitation as a binding goal. This is no longer achievable due to the global »Tipping Point«, isn't it?

STEVEN FISSLER

In all likelihood, not any more. Now that the »Tipping Point« has occurred, global society would be well advised to do everything possible to still achieve the goal of a maximum global temperature increase of 2.0° Celsius compared to the pre-industrial value. That is actually at least 0.5° Celsius too much, because an increase of more than 1.5 °Celsius will lead to many islands and island states to be drowned. Unfortunately, the latest climate simulations show unequivocally that by the end of this century, significantly more than 2.0°Celsius of global temperature increase is likely. It could be 3.0° to 6.0° Celsius more. Some parts of the world are threatened with temperatures so high that they will become uninhabitable.

Perhaps we, humankind, will succeed in making many, many small and some very large attempts to combat global warming. Then things may be different.

BETTINA ROLAND

For these reasons, every initiative, no matter how small, that counteracts the »Tipping Point« is enormously important.

FRANK RAUTER

There is really no alternative to this! We must drastically reduce greenhouse gas emissions to not further deteriorate our quality of life and to retain a world worth living in for our children, grandchildren and future generations.

STEVEN FISSLER

It is imperative to reduce the global CO2 concentration in the atmosphere. We must bear in mind that in 1990 global CO2 emissions were still 22.5 billion tonnes, in 2015 it already was just under 36 billion tonnes. Since then emissions of CO2 continued to rise annually by between 600 and 800 million tonnes. This is mainly because the countries in the Northern Hemisphere still produce too much CO2. Add to this India, the most populous country on earth, which is booming enormously economically and therefore produces much more C02 than fifteen or twenty years ago. Likewise, China's economic growth rates remain high. Since the turn of the millennium at the latest, large African countries and Indonesia, for example, have also been adopting more and more of the Western lifestyle. We know that this is mainly not only a further waste of resources, but also produces far too much additional CO2 emissions.

PAULA SPITERI

The future of our children and the generations to come largely depends on us learning to manage the climate so that we produce fewer greenhouse gas emissions; we have to take actions against the many extreme weather events and rising sea levels.

BETTINA ROLAND

Since you refer to attempts at solutions that could help improve life with the »Tipping Point« what exactly do you mean by taking actions? Can you go into more details?

PAULA SPITERI

For instance, raising dykes as water protection on river and sea banks is urgently needed. Extensions and adjustments to dams and rivers as well as the renaturation of riverbeds must be carried out. Furthermore, significant quality improvements and rehabilitation work on existing dykes and dams must be provided. Also importantly, a significant reduction in energy and resource consumption must be realised, because ultimately this is the only way to reduce CO2 production. The necessary steps must be taken by all countries worldwide as part of the so-called 'development cooperation'. The economic invested in measures against the effects of climate change will pay off hundredfold.

FRANK RAUTER

These findings were emphasised again and again at the last world climate summits, but have been followed far too half-heartedly so far. If the efforts by world leaders to tackle the obvious issues continue to be conducted so poorly, in the not too distant future many more climate refugees will come from the central and Equator regions to the North and South. The most frequent causes of people fleeing their home countries are still civil wars and displacement. But more and more people are fleeing from Africa and Asia because of devastating environmental conditions that cause hunger and great poverty and are ultimately the result of climate change.

By the way, in 2010 a significant proportion of refugees seeking asylum in Europe left for climate related reasons.

PAULA SPITERI

From 2007 to 2010, Iraq and Syria for example experienced the worst drought in a hundred years on top of wars going on. Because the land withered, the rural population moved towards the cities which became unbearably crowded. A struggle for jobs ensued. Water too became scarce and expensive. The great drought in this region was the result of global warming and aggravated the civil war that had already begun. So, the refugees from Iraq and Syria were not only war refugees but also climate refugees. We shall not send back people who claim a valid reason for fleeing their home.

PRODUCER

Some statistics about life expectancy…

VOICE OVER

Average life expectancy in Australia has fallen significantly due to climate change. According to ABS statistics the average life expectancy in 2019 was 80.7 years for the males and 84.9 for females. The latest figures are 78.9 years for men and 83 years for females. There are no specific numbers for the non-binary community.

PAULA SPITERI

Calculations by renowned non-governmental organisations predict that around 250 million people could become climate refugees. People will flee because their countries are only just above sea level, such as populous Bangladesh. Or people will flee because they live on islands that are more or less submerged by rising sea levels. It is curious that under international law there are actually no climate refugees because the Geneva Refugee Convention still does not provide for climate refugees. Ultimately, climate refugees should have the same right to asylum as war refugees.

JOSEPH MOLDEN

It's good the way it is, otherwise, even more refugees would come to Australia, and we had to intern them on other islands too before finally officially deporting them. The boat is full.

MIA SCHELLINGER/FRANK RAUTER

(loudly in protest) Disgraceful! Intolerable! If there are any small islands left at all.

PRODUCER

STOP – CUT!!! Short break!

BETTINA ROLAND

Sorry Minister, in your position you should not make such statements.

JOSEPH MOLDEN

Yes, I shall, especially here, where many people see and hear me. Hopefully many people from Africa and Asia too.

FRANK RAUTER

That is populism. With this statement you bluntly aim at votes on the right.

JOSEPH MOLDEN

Our party is in the political center. Let's be clear about that!

PRODUCER

Let's listen to a new announcement.

VOICE OVER

CO2 emissions have caused an over-acidification of the world's oceans that has never been recorded. The over-acidification has never been so great in the course of the last 300 million years. As a result, coral reefs worldwide are acutely threatened. Acidification is the cause of the extinction of thirty percent of marine life. (Mia Schellinger indicates that she wants to speak.)

BETTINA ROLAND

Mia, you wanted to say something.

MIA SCHELLINGER

Yes, I absolutely need to clarify something about the Minister's statements: The climate refugees who come to us have contributed the least to global warming through their lifestyles. They have generally not benefitted from economic growth either. But they have to pay with the loss of their homeland under the consequences of the growth mania, which has contributed significantly to global warming. You should be ashamed of your statement, Minister. It is a disgrace that you are in this show and using it for your political slender. I feel sick having to share this space with you. Shit, shit, shit!

FRANK RAUTER

I repeat myself. You belong before a tribunal.

BETTINA ROLAND

Frank, please refrain from such personal verbal attacks in my show. You got it! You too, Mia Schellinger, watch what you are saying. Thank you.

FRANK RAUTER

Yes, but I guess it is still allowed to be angry and comment on such bullshit.

BETTINA ROLAND

But not like that! Minister, I apologize for Frank Rauter's comments.

MIA SCHELLINGER

Well Bettina, I will be silent from now on.

JOSEPH MOLDEN

You are not only an aggressive stirrer but also a lout. You will pay for what you said. I will see to that. First thing Monday I will sue you for public insult.

WALTER MILLERT

Joseph, I will join you in that because I have also been insulted during this show. And you, Ms Roland, should have a hard look at yourself about the choice of people you invite to your talk show.

BETTINA ROLAND

I do hope you won't want to tell me how to do my job. Please stop bickering here in front of our audience. Let's move on.

Ms Spiteri, you haven't finished your earlier comments yet.

JOSEPH MOLDEN

Bickering would be all right. I wouldn't object to that, but I and Mr. Millert here have been accused of special culpability for the »Tipping Point«.

BETTINA ROLAND

I don't think that's right either. So, Paula Spiteri - please.

PAULA SPITERI

Yes, but firstly I wish to point out that Mia Schellinger's response to Minister Molden's statement in the context of climate refugees is correct. I hope that I won't be sued too for expressing this opinion.

Okay, let's move on. I just wanted to say that another precautionary measure should be launched in the form of resettling people who already today and in the foreseeable future will no longer be able to live on their land because of rising sea levels. Preparations for resettlement measures should also be massively supported as part of so-called development cooperation. Perhaps climate refugees from our neighboring islands in the Pacific have to be resettled in Queensland. Well, Minister Molden, you should prepare for this.

JOSEPH MOLDEN

Now even you are changing tone. I didn't expect that.

PAULA SPITERI

Are you going to report me on Monday too?

JOSEPH MOLDEN

No. No reason for that.

PAULA SPITERI

Well, I must say I'm quite relieved. Steven.

BETTINA ROLAND

You wanted to say something else, Professor Fissler?

STEVEN FISSLER

Yes, I would add to Ms Spiteri's precautionary measures that we also have to create huge overflow regions so that less water can reach the cities due to the rising sea level and the even further increasing heavy rainfall events on the one hand or water can also be drained away from the cities better on the other. It could also become possible that in some countries we will have to move away from the coastal regions al together, i.e. virtually abandon coastal cities.

That is why the flood protection you described, Ms Spiteri, is so enormously important. Incidentally, we should seek advice and action for sustainable flood protection from the Dutch. The Netherlands are the absolute world leaders in flood protection.

FRANK RAUTER

If we succeed in climate control and precaution, our grandchildren and greatgrandchildren can look back on us with pride. If it fails, they will rightly condemn us.

MIA SCHELLINGER

But despite all these very hard facts and the declining quality of life due to climate change, material growth is still being generated everywhere in the world at all costs and on all possible levels! By this I mean that artificial needs are constantly being created, which further exacerbate the many crises and catastrophes. A turnaround in growth is long overdue at the global level!

**PRODUCER –
VOICE OVER**

May 2029 was the warmest on record worldwide, meteorologists from the US climate agency NOAA announced today.

BETTINA ROLAND

Paula …

PAULA SPITERI

What Mia Schellinger said is absolutely right. We urgently need to turn away from the current capitalism, including the complete abandonment of the fossil economy, i.e. energy production from coal, natural gas and oil. The dismantling of the fossil economy pursued so far and the share of renewable energy sources in total energy consumption achieved to date are far from sufficient. Even Pope Francis made a drastic reminder of this in his environmental encyclical in 2015. Pope Francis spoke out against mankind's current way of life, which he described as »suicidal«. Never before has humanity treated the environment as badly as it did in the and 19th and 20th Century. The earth seems to be developing into an »immeasurable landfill«. Global warming in particular is »one of the most important challenges facing humanity today«, which is why it is of great importance to drastically reduce greenhouse gas emissions and to stop burning fossil fuels.

WALTER MILLERT

Now I would finally like to say something.

PAULA SPITERI

Mr Millert, please let me finish first. I don't interrupt you when you are speaking.

PRODUCER
(signales camera and sound to stop)

WALTER MILLERT

You couldn't interrupt me either because I have said almost nothing so far.

BETTINA ROLAND

Now, nevertheless, Ms Spiteri should continue to speak.

PRODUCER

Camera, Sound!

PAULA SPITERI

I just wanted to emphasise that the overexploitation of the biosphere must be stopped urgently. I say this not because I am an evolutionary biologist and ecologist, but as a mother of two children whose future I see as very much under threat. Due to the climate change we have caused and our overexploitation of nature, not only are many animal species already extinct or acutely endangered. More than a fifth of all plant species are threatened with extinction. For example, around ninety percent of wheat, maize and tomato varieties have been lost in recent decades. Since the 1980s, far more than twenty per cent of tropical forests have been cleared. An area equivalent to thirty-five football fields of tropical rainforest is destroyed every minute. This also destroys countless animal and plant species. A disgrace that cannot be put into words.

MIA SCHELLINGER

Rainforest is being destroyed for the cultivation of soy for concentrated feed for farm animals; Brazil is one of the world's largest exporters of beef. Large areas of rainforest are being cleared to make room for pasture.

Rainforest is also cleared for palm oil plantations. On the islands of Sumatra and Kalimantan, the Indonesian part of Borneo, rainforest is being destroyed by illegal slash-and-burn. Plantation owners and farmers burn their land every year during the dry season to create space for new cultivation areas, including palm oil. With the giant trees cleared, rare and beautiful animals such as orangutans, tigers and rhinos are becoming extinct. If their habitat continues to be cut down in this way, they could soon disappear completely. Many primeval forests in Indonesia, the world export champion for palm oil, are so-called peat bog forests. A particularly large amount of CO_2 is stored in them. When these forests are cleared, it is released and contributes massively to global warming. Slash-and-burn clearing produces even more CO_2. Rainforests are also destroyed for tropical timber, biodiesel, aluminium, gold and much more.

The most obscene development in Borneo was when in 2019 the Indonesian Government decided to build their new Capital City »Nusantara« in the East Kalimantan province of Borneo against the will of the people destroying more than 200,000 ha of inland forest, almost three-times the size of New York City! Why, the government claimed it was necessary because their previous capital city Jakarta was often flooded and traffic-choked.

These kinds of worldwide destruction of nature have to be stopped.

STEVEN FISSLER

If this were achieved, it would be a very big step towards reversing the »Tipping Point«.

**PRODUCER –
VOICE OVER**

Today, shops were again brutally looted in some Australian cities. This year there have already been more lootings of shops than in the whole of last year. The looters come from all social backgrounds. More and more women and children are taking part. In the shops, drinks of all kinds are looted, but no cash-registers, sweets or other valuables. The beverage stocks of the shops are usually completely stripped by the looters. For the transport more and more stolen vans are used. The Australian Government has been demanding increased protection for shops for some time and will discuss the issue next Monday. The costs for this are to be passed on to the price of these drinks.

BETTINA ROLAND

Back to our discussion.

JOSEPH MOLDEN

Ms Schellinger, Ms Spiteri, I fully agree and support what you just said. The Australian Government has already done a lot to reinforce the protection of rainforests. But the multinationals repeatedly evade compliance with laws and the strict guidelines and regulations for sustainable and fair products. They produce in countries where especially the laws and regulations for sustainable and fair production do not apply.

MIA SCHELLINGER

Products must be much better labelled with sustainable quality seals and fair working conditions. And products that do not comply with this shall not being imported into Australia.

JOSEPH MOLDEN

Well, it is so easy to claim in theory, but generally impossible to realize in our globalized world.

FRANK RAUTER

This is also a challenge for consumers. They have to pay more attention to sustainable and fair products. But for this, the products must be much better labelled, as Mia just pointed out.

PAULA SPITERI

Thank you Ms Schellinger for your expert comments.

BETTINA ROLAND

Ms Schellinger, I appreciate your wealth of knowledge which you have at your fingertips.

STEVEN FISSLER

Me too, especially as you are still so young.

MIA SCHELLINGER

These were just a few details about the destruction of the rain-forests. I could name many more facts.

FRANK RAUTER

What are we going to tell our children? We are leaving them a world without a future. Or is anyone here of a different opinion?

PRODUCER
(signals urgently to Bettina to chance the subject)

BETTINA ROLAND

I reckon, we should only talk about solutions now for the rest of the show.

We shall now use the remaining time to point out positive thoughts about how we can deal with this epochal crisis. We must continue to talk about ways to help prevent the crises caused by increasing global warming from getting worse. We shall outline prospects how the consequences of global warming could be partially or eventually completely solved. We owe this to the many millions of viewers.

FRANK RAUTER

I am not happy, Bettina, that you simply ignored my last statement and question.

BETTINA ROLAND

Let's spend the rest of the show discussing the fact that our world doesn't have to be futureless, shall we?

MIA SCHELLINGER

But it will become futureless if we do not get our act together now and start reversing uncontrolled growth on all levels.

BETTINA ROLAND

By the way, »Degrowth« means »growth reversal« or »growth turnaround«. Is that right, Ms Schellinger?

MIA SCHELLIINGER

Correct…

BETTINA ROLAND

Since you have been a quite successful activist for a long time can you please explain your philosophy and inherit core demands or those of the Degrowth-Movement. These certainly include solutions to mitigate the consequences of the »Tipping Point«.

**PRODUCER –
VOICE OVER**

The nearly twelve hundred islands of the Maldives are under increasingly acute threat because of rising sea levels. The Maldivian government today appealed to the rich countries to provide as much aid as possible for precautionary measures to limit the effects of climate change on the Maldivian islands. For many years, precautionary measures have cost the Maldives more than half of its budget. The Maldives now spends as much on measures against dam erosion as it does on education and health. Many islanders have already been resettled for years because of the rising sea levels. There are seventy islands in the Maldives struggling with contaminated water. Salt water is leaking into the drinking water system and more and more islands are losing surface area due to erosion.

BETTINA ROLAND

So, Mia – your turn.

MIA SCHELLINGER

First of all, I would like to say that all the following points are equally important and closely interlinked. So, taxes on aeroplane travel and the whole energy and resource consumption must be much higher to reduce CO2 emissions and save resources. The resulting tax revenues should be invested in sustainability projects. Hidden social and environmental costs must be included in the prices of products. The local economy must be massively promoted fiscally and legally to create short transport routes, strengthened rural areas and much more transparency in production. The privatisation of public goods must be completely reversed.

Common goods are particularly important to the Degrowth-Movement, which is why they must not be privatised. From water to energy supply to housing, these should be available to the public at an affordable price. The public should take over the management of these.

We also need to invest much more in public infrastructure. Instead of pouring an enormous amount of money into prestigious public buildings or road construction, the state should promote public transport and the infrastructure for cycling and walking. That would make our cities more liveable. They would become quieter because fewer cars would drive in them. They would become healthier because far fewer exhaust emissions would be released, to name just two of many hundreds of benefits. The restructuring of the infrastructure must be pushed forward.

Instead of always building new bypasses and ring-road systems that create incentives to use the car, the existing infrastructure must be used more efficiently. Environmentally unfriendly tax breaks must be eliminated, such as for company cars and aviation fuel. These provide the wrong incentives and create unnecessary demand. Of course, education also needs to be reformed. The curriculum must include education about all environmental problems and climate change. Environmental education has to start in kindergarten. The sealing of land for streets, commercial buildings, airports and ever increasing extension of residential areas in Australia must be stopped urgently and green spaces must be preserved. As far as possible, areas should be unsealed and used for biotopes and trees. Unsealed areas are good for the climate in several ways.

STEVEN FISSLER

Ms Schellinger, absolutely agree with all of it. Most of the issues were already listed in the 1970s and early 1980s. How does the practical impact the Degrowth-Movement has look like, though?

MIA SCHELLINGER

The difference between the theoretical concepts, which have admittedly been around for a long time, and the practical realization is that this form of growth turnaround is already being lived out in countless projects all over the world. The individual concepts for this are adapted and refined day by day to the respective conditions. This also includes the Transition Town movement. It exists in over five hundred places in more than fifty countries. Each Transition Town, i.e. an entire city or just a neighbourhood, commits to action plans designed to reduce energy consumption. These are always joint plans to reduce emissions and wean themselves off fossil fuels. This is a very important contribution against global warming. Moreover, the followers of the Degrowth-Movement avoid any form of mass-consumption and unnecessary use of energy and resources. They, therefore, have an extremely good CO_2 balance, meaning, they produce about 80% less CO_2 per capita than the average population.

BETTINA ROLAND

Thank you very much, Mia Schellinger. Now a short interruption of the discussion for a small informative interlude with a question to the studio audience. (She stands up and walks to the edge of the studio or the stage and directs her gaze towards the studio audience or the theatre audience.)

So, dear audience members here in the studio: Do you also use a CO2 app on your smartwatches or slightly older smartphone models? (She waits a few seconds and then announces the result.)

This app measures everything you produce in CO2, including the almost 0.8 tons of CO2 emissions per person for a return flight from Melbourne to Brisbane or the approx. 9.6 tons of CO2 emissions per person for a return flight from Melbourne to New York; they even measure all the CO2 emissions created in the manufacture of the products they purchase. It measures the CO2 production of their car and train miles, of their home, the food they eat and much more.

STEVEN FISSLER

I would like to point out that a scientific model shows that to still be deemed climate-friendly CO2 production per person must not exceed 2,3 tons per year.

MIA SCHELLINGER

Then the supporters of the Degrowth-Movement are behaving in a climate-friendly way because in Australia the CO2 production per capita and year is on average 15.01 tons according to STATISTA. This includes babies and small children. In contrast, the CO2 production per capita for the participants in the Degrowth-Movement is only a little over two tons on average. Therefore they - obviously - live a climate-friendly life.

WALTER MILLERT

Has this been independently determined and verified?

MIA SCHELLINGER

You won't believe it, yes! There was an independent study for Australia in 2028 commissioned by our government. The CO2 production per capita for degrowth supporters that I stated was determined in this study.

WALTER MILLERT

Thank you.

FRANK RAUTER

Mia, what the Degrowth-Movement is doing is just brilliant.

BETTINA ROLAND

Thank you for this extremely important information, Professor Fissler, and for your detailed facts, Ms Spichtinger.

JOSEPH MOLDEN

Ms Roland, you must have a CO2 app on your beautiful smart-watch. Why don't you tell us how much CO2 you produced in the last twelve months.

BETTINA ROLAND

I see. Yes, Minister, I've had a CO2 app for about two years now. Well, in the last few months I have produced a relatively large amount I have to admit. In view of the »Tipping Point« I surely have to reduce my carbon-footprint significantly.

JOSEPH MOLDEN

But you can give us a figure for the CO2 emissions you cause, can you?

BETTINA ROLAND

Well, to be honest I have produced over forty tons of CO2 in the last twelve months, forty-three to be precise. If I were to mention a lower value here, it would surely made public by the tabloid press the day after tomorrow at the latest, because my smartwatch data cannot be kept secret. As a journalist, I have to fly a lot as the whole world knows. But I have had all my flights made climate-neutral through CO2 offsetting. I can prove that. The compensation money is used to build up renewable energies. The company that carries out these services is certified and is strictly audited on a regular basis.

JOSEPH MOLDEN

Despite the compensation fees paid you are not a role model, though.

BETTINA ROLAND

I never said that.

JOSEPH MOLDEN

O.K. I admit as a politician I also travel a lot. My CO2 emissions are probably similarly high, and have been for years.

FRANK RAUTER

Bettina, your CO2 emissions are really far too high.

MIA SCHELLINGER

See, almost everyone has excuses and arguments as to why they are excessively prone to produce CO2-emissions. Everyone should take the people of the Degrowth-Movement as a role-model! If energy were much more expensive per se, large amounts of CO2 could be avoided. But even this simple control instrument has not been used politically so far.

JOSEPH MOLDEN

It is not that easy to regulate energy prices in our globalised world. To achieve this, many countries would have to join in.

MIA SCHELLINGER

But this is the core responsibility of politics, of politicians, to make sure that something like this can be achieved.

WALTER MILLERT

But the economic competitiveness, especially in view of India, China and Brazil would suffer. Mass unemployment would be the result.

FRANK RAUTER

You don't get it, Mr Millert, nothing at all.

MIA SCHELLINGER

All countries must get out of the global markets and into national, regional markets. That would defuse many crises. Then energy could be taxed in a completely different way.

JOSEPH MOLDEN

Why don't you go into politics to implement such things? You will quickly learn that this can only be done with a lot of patience and with very small political steps. But you also need many supporters for this, here in Australia and in many countries.

MIA SCHELLINGER

However, due to the »Tipping Point«, there is no time left for playing politics, politicians must now act quickly.

JOSEPH MOLDEN

I do not dispute that at all, my government will act quickly.

BETTINA ROLAND

Thank you, Ms Schellinger, thank you Minister. Mr Molden, I am sure you will certainly make a statement about what the Federal Government will do about the »Tipping Point«.

WALTER MILLERT

Sorry, before we come to that I really want to draw your attention to an important issue that has not been mentioned so far.

BETTINA ROLAND

Thank you Mr. Millert. Please enlighten us; we are all curious to learn about your constructive ideas.

WALTER MILLERT

I have now listened patiently to everything that has been said so far, especially Professor Fissler's detailed explanations. There are completely different reasons for the climate change. The claim about the so called »Tipping Point« made by the Intergovernmental Panel on Climate Change on Monday is nothing but a conspiracy formula against the global economy. Humans are not the cause of global warming, because the climate has always been changing. The Intergovernmental Panel on Climate Change is clearly engaged in scaremongering here, and on Monday in Paris it put the world community in a state of alarm – recklessly and totally unwarranted. I suspect that the solar industry, the wind power manufacturers and the alternative movement are trying to pull the wool over its eyes. They probably want to disband the existing social order. The scientists of the Intergovernmental Panel on Climate Change are deliberately exaggerating the climate risks. More than five hundred scientists from many countries doubt that the greenhouse effect was exacerbated by human activity. Anyone can read about this on the internet and find many good arguments that support this fact.

Because of the current global warming, which is based on natural causes, we can't completely question the fossil economy as such. If we did, our future would be truly threatened.

BETTINA ROLAND

Mr Millert, I expected a constructive contribution to the discussion – your statement was definitely a quite unpleasant surprise.

STEVEN FISSLER

The arguments against the fact that human activity is responsible for the rapid climate change that have been posted on the internet are scientifically baseless. Many of the names of the signatories on those websites and Facebook posts are fictitious or forged. Even my name can be found there and I have already called my lawyer to follow up the abuse of my identity. Some colleagues I know very well are also wrongly and criminally quoted to support these untenable arguments. They have also started legal action. Like me, they are convinced that climate change with the consequence of additional global warming has been and is being caused by us humans because the evidence is overwhelming. These baseless arguments against man-made climate change must be removed from the net at all costs as it is not about the right to free speech here but criminal deception – it's about them pulling wool over the public's eyes.

I also object to your assertion that the Intergovernmental Panel on Climate Change is conspiring against the global economy. It is not engaged in scaremongering, nor is it being roped in for any political agenda by anyone.

PRODUCER –
VOICE OVER

Today the International Tourism Federation announced climate tourism to Iceland, which has grown substantially in recent years, has already seen significant growth this year despite substantial increases in the cost of airfares and accommodation. Tourism to Iceland is particularly favoured by the upper middle class to escape the heat for a few days or for the entire holiday period. Comparable increases can also be reported from the USA. There, more and more holiday flights to Canada and Alaska are being booked to escape the summer heat.

PAULA SPITERI

It's crazy. In the past, holidays were booked to enjoy a sunny and warm environment. Today, holidays to cooler countries are preferred, even though these trips contribute to the generation of even more CO2 emissions, which will speeding up, hence worsen the global warming.

FRANK RAUTER

With the »Tipping Point« reached, such trips should become so expensive that they no longer affordable.

MIA SCHELLINGER

A drastic price increase should be made for air travel in general and for cruises, and that through the tax system. This cannot be achieved in any other way.

BETTINA ROLAND

Well, Mr Molden, now it's your turn.

JOSEPH MOLDEN

Yes, thank you. Here I have to agree with Walter Millert at least on the point that there has always been climate change. Also, based on a representative poll conducted on Thursday fifty-five per cent of respondents do not believe in man-made global warming. People think global warming is a natural climate fluctuation.

STEVEN FISSLER

Well, we have to ask who was the initiator of this »representative poll« and who were the people who responded. In any case, this survey only reflects opinions, but it cannot change the undoubtedly scientifically proven conclusion that global warming is caused by us humans.

FRANK RAUTER

You are beyond salvation, Millert. How dare you spreading such nonsense. You should be ashamed of yourself, because you know you are talking nonsense. Especially as a top politician, Minister Molden, you should not side with the climate sceptics.

JOSEPH MOLDEN

I am not – actually.

MIA SCHELLINGER

Such people control the fortunes of large corporations. They think only of profit and say to themselves: Let the devil take the hindmost. They are really jointly responsible for the destruction of the foundations of life on earth.

BETTINA ROLAND

You don't always have to shout like that, Mia! We can understand you anyway.

STEVEN FISSLER

I don't want to downplay anything here, but don't most people in the more prosperous countries live by the maxim »After me, the deluge«?

FRANK RAUTER

Consumer mentality and leisure behaviour of the wider community suggests exactly that.

MIA SCHELLINGER

»After me, the deluge« is probably what our climate sceptic Millert thinks, the CEO of an energy company that still relies on coal, gas and oil. It's horrible. I'm leaving now. I can't sit here anymore. Frank, are you coming?

FRANK RAUTER

Yes, I'll come along. People like Millert and Molden belong before a tribunal and not on this show. They have played a major role in the destruction of the earth. Bastards!

BETTINA ROLAND

You can't speak like that! You'll never get an invitation to my talk show again.

Dear viewers in Australia and all over the world, dear studio audience, dear guests: that is the essence of a live show. As you have seen, some guests also have a really bad day and are not on their best behaviour.

Before we continue, I would like to ask the studio audience: Who shares the opinion that climate change is not caused by human actions for at least in the last 250 years? Please show hands.

We are nearing the end of the show. So far, we have heard little from our Federal Minister for Economy and Energy about what he, or rather the Federal Government, is going to do about the »Tipping Point«. And Walter Millert, who is after all CEO of Sydney based Energypower Group Ltd and has a huge responsibility, owes us all an answer as to how he will convert his company to renewable energy.

Who of you, Ms Spiteri and Professor Fissler, would like to ask Minister Joseph Molden a final question on this? Your statement will be neither commented on nor discussed.

STEVEN FISSLER

Minister, what concrete actions will the Australian government take immediately at national and international level to meet the challenges of the »Tipping Points«. My emphasis is on immediate action. Since the 2015 global climate agreement, the Australian Government has done virtually nothing nationally and internationally to address global warming, nothing to meet the target of a maximum of 1.5°C of additional global warming over pre-industrial levels. Australia still relies on coal and gas as if there was no man-made global warming. Australia is by far the largest exporter of coal. The expansion of all forms of renewable energy has also been more than half-hearted so far. This is very bad especially since Australia like few other countries in the world isa particularly effected by increasing global warming. Every year in Australia we have more and more bushfires, longer and longer periods of drought and heat waves and more and more weather anomalies in general. This year, as we have experienced there were more than 100 major fires in the state of NSW alone, burning an area larger than Austria. On top of that, corals are dying in the World Heritage Site 'Great Barrier Reef'. In the latest CLIMATE PROTECTION INDEX of the organization German Watch, Australia comes in 54th place out of 61 countries surveyed – only seven countries have a worse climate protection record than Australia.

JOSEPH MOLDEN

I acknowledge that Australian governments have underestimated the dangers of global warming for several decades. As an immediate measure the Australian Government wants to quickly reaffirm the pledges to the existing global climate treaty. To do this, it will significantly increase financial contributions to developing countries and emerging economies for climate protection actions of all kinds. In Australia we will introduce an array of policies to achieve the reduction of unnecessary energy consumption in private and business settings. Remaining private transport using fossil fuels will be heavily taxed from 2030.

In addition, we want to increase regenerative energy production much more and discuss and introduce incentives to safe energy socially. The stalled electro-mobility and the expansion and quality of local and long distance passenger transport should also be drastically boosted.

PAULA SPITERI

Mr Molden, we knew long before the »Tipping Point« that coal, gas and oil are the worst climate killers. Why does the Australian Government still not have a plan to phase out coal and gas mining as the Federal Republic of Germany does, for example? The Greens have been demanding this for years. And why does Australia still export the climate killer coal to many countries and thus actively contribute to further global warming?

JOSEPH MOLDEN

We have only known since Monday that the »Tipping Point« has occurred. Having learnt about the latest development we immediately decided on the measures just outlined.
However, if we were to abandon coal mining as Germany has done, for example, it would be a revolution for Australia with incalculable consequences for our economy. Not only would we lose hundreds of thousands of jobs but a great deal of our revenue. But I acknowledge that in view of our 2050 commitments we need to discuss a possible phase-out of coal sometime.

PAULA SPITERI

What you offer in the face of the »Tipping Point« is far too little. The Australian Government should develop a plan to quickly phase out coal mining without any undue delay and massively expand capacities for renewable energy sources.

JOSEPH MOLDEN

That's what I will be campaigning for from Monday on. But despite the »Tipping Point« a switch from coal and gas to renewable energy only will take technically a long time.

BETTINA ROLAND

But we expect that you and the Government shall acknowledge that action has to be taken immediately.

STEVEN FISSLER

For aviation and shipping, there are still no targets to reduce their CO2 emissions since the Paris Climate Agreement came into force because this could not be built into the agreement. The lobbyists were successful in preventing this. Is the Australian Government now also taking action in this regard?

JOSEPH MOLDEN

It is not ministerial responsibilities to decide that, but of course I will work for it

STEVEN FISSLER

It is clear that Australia should quickly phase out coal and gas mining and, at the same time, make considerable energy savings. It is also clear that Australia needs to start a huge structural change and intensively increase renewable energy. The old jobs from the fossil industries need to be replaced by new jobs for the solar power and windfarm industries. In addition, many new jobs can be created by transforming non-sustainable production into truly sustainable production. Every Australian, regardless of their social background and from all professions should become actively involved in that societal and economic transformation.

The situation is very serious but a livable future can still be secured.

BETTINA ROLAND

Thank you very much, Professor Fissler; that was a fitting closing statement.

We are at the end of our show. A big Thankyou to our panel. Of course, I would also like to thank the studio audience and the many millions of viewers around the world. I believe that we have got valuable insight into the complex tropic. We now know a bit more about what led to the »Tipping Point« and more about what possibilities there are to preserve the future viability of human civilisation despite the »Tipping Point«. We also know that the Australian Government must act quickly and that the Australian people will also be challenged to do their bit to tackle the problem.

We have seen a lively and passionate discussion and I am confident we could contribute to a positive outlook into the future. I look forward to seeing you again next week when we discuss another interesting topic.

PRODUCER

Thank you, team – wrap up.

Many thanks to you - our studio audience; the show we have just recorded will be aired in Australia the day after tomorrow at 7:30 pm Australian Eastern Standard Time and at the respective local times throughout our network.

End of stage performance

Projection of the start of the recorded show

BETTINA. ROLAND

Good evening, ladies and gentlemen here in the studio and wherever you follow this show out there.

The whole world has been talking about the »Tipping Point« since Monday. On Monday, the Intergovernmental Panel on Climate Change rated the accuracy of the»Tipping Point« as highly probable. This means that climate change has reached the so-called »point of no return«. According to the Intergovernmental Panel on Climate Change, this means that global society will be exposed to climate change with even further increasing global warming and the resulting negative consequences for a longer period of time, because the global climate has tipped. The earth continues to warm up without us humans being able to do anything about it in the short term. Counter measures that lead to a reduction in global warming would only have a positive effect several generations later, according to the Intergovernmental Panel on Climate Change. My guests are here today to talk with me about this very disturbing finding. They have been chosen to share their different professional backgrounds and knowledge of the most important causes leading to the »Tipping Point«.

In particular, they are joining us tonight to discuss possibilities of how we can maintain or perhaps even improve our quality of life despite the considerable difficulties caused by the changing climate. Let me first welcome Evolutionary Biologist and Ecologist Paula Spiteri. She is known far beyond Australia's borders through her TV-Programs and successful books on Nature and Species' Conservation many of which have won awards…

Curtain Call

Background literature and research sources

Franziskus (Papst) (2015). *Gebet für unsere Erde. Aus der Enzyklika »Laudato si«.* Freiburg: Herder.

Germanwatch (2022). Klimaschutz-Index 2022: Die wichtigsten Ergebnisse. Abgerufen am 15.02.2022, von https://www.germanwatch.org/de/21110.

Graßl, Hartmut und Reiner Klingholz (1990): *Wir Klimamacher. Auswege aus dem globalen Treibhaus.* Frankfurt/Main: S. Fischer.

Graßl, Hartmut (1999). *Wetterwende. Vision: Globaler Klimaschutz.* Frankfurt/Main: Campus.

Intergovernmental Panel on Climate Change (2021). Climate Change 2021. The Physical Science Basis. Summary for Policymakers. Abgerufen am 06.12.2021, von https://www.ipcc.ch/report/ar6/wg1/downloads/report/IPCC_AR6_WGISPM_final.pdf#page=33.

IPCC Deutsche Koordinierungsstelle (2021). IPCC: Zwischenstaatlicher Ausschuss für Klimaänderungen. Abgerufen am 05.12.2021, von https://www.de-ipcc.de/119.php.

IPCC Deutsche Koordinierungsstelle (2021). Sechster IPCC-Sachstandsbericht (AR6), Beitrag von Arbeitsgruppe I: Naturwissenschaftliche Grundlagen. Abgerufen am 13.12.2021, von https://www.de-ipcc.de/media/content/IPCC-AR6-WGI_Hauptaussagen_deutsch.pdf.

Klein. Naomi (2015). *Die Entscheidung. Kapitalismus vs. Klima.* Frankfurt/Main: S. Fischer.

Latif, Mojib (2005). »Verändert der Mensch das Klima?« In: Die Zukunft der Erde. Was verträgt unser Planet noch? Hg. Ernst Peter Fischer und Klaus Wiegandt, Frankfurt/Main: Fischer Taschenbuch Verlag.

Latif, Mojib (2020). *Heisszeit. Mit Vollgas in die Klimakatastrophe – und wie wir auf die Bremse treten.* Freiburg im Breisgau: Herder.

Mittelstaedt, Werner (1988): *Wachstumswende. Chance für die Zukunft.* München: Wirtschaftsverlag Langen-Müller/Herbig.

Mittelstaedt, Werner (1993). *Zukunftsgestaltung und Chaostheorie. Grundlagen einer neuen Zukunftsgestaltung unter Einbeziehung der Chaostheorie.* Frankfurt/Main et al.: Peter Lang.

Mittelstaedt, Werner (1997). *Der Chaos-Schock und die Zukunft der Menschheit.* Frankfurt/Main et al.: Peter Lang.

Mittelstaedt, Werner (2000). *Frieden, Wissenschaft, Zukunft 21. Visionen für das neue Jahrhundert.* Frankfurt/Main et al.: Peter Lang.

Mittelstaedt, Werner (2004*). Kurskorrektur. Bausteine für die Zukunft.* Frankfurt/Main: Edition Büchergilde.

Mittelstaedt, Werner (2008). *Das Prinzip Fortschritt 21. Ein neues Verständnis für die Herausforderungen unserer Zeit.* Frankfurt/Main et al.: Peter Lang.

Mittelstaedt, Werner (2012): *SMALL. Warum weniger besser ist und was wir dazu wissen sollten.* Frankfurt/Main et al.: Peter Lang.

Mittelstaedt, Werner (2020). *Anthropozän und Nachhaltigkeit. Denkanstöße zur Klimakrise und für ein zukunftsfähiges Handeln.* Berlin et al.: Peter Lang.

MPI und DKRZ (1992). Das Klima der nächsten hundert Jahre (VHS-PAL Video). Hamburg: Max-Planck-Institut für Meteorologie (MPI) und Deutsches Klimarechenzentrum (DKRZ).

MPI und DKRZ (1995). Klimasimulationen – Vorhersage des globalen Wandels (VHS-PAL Video). Hamburg: Max-Planck-Institut für Meteorologie (MPI) und Deutsches Klimarechenzentrum (DKRZ).

Scheer, Hermann (2010*). Der energethische Imperativ. 100 Prozent jetzt: Wie der vollständige Wechsel zu erneuerbaren Energien zu realisieren ist.* München: Kunstmann.

Schellnhuber, Hans Joachim (2006). »Kipp-Punkte im Erdsystem. Interview mit Hans Joachim Schellnhuber, Direktor des Potsdam-Instituts für Klimaforschung«. Internet: ww.germanwatch.org/rio/hjsint06.pdf.

Smolin, Lee (2014). *Im Universum der Zeit. Auf dem Weg zu einem neuen Verständnis des Kosmos.* München: Deutsche Verlags-Anstalt.

Walker, Gabrielle und David King (2008*). Ganz heiss Die Herausforderungen des Klimawandels.* Berlin: Berlin Verlag.

Weizsäcker, Ernst Ulrich von et al. (2010). *Faktor Fünf. Die Formel für nachhaltiges Wachstum.* München: Droemer

Wissenschaftlicher Beirat der Bundesregierung Globale Umweltveränderungen (WBGU) (2009). Welt im Wandel. Zukunftsfähige Bioenergie und nachhaltige Landnutzung. Berlin: WBGU.

Wobben, Aloys (2009). »Das friedensstiftende Potential der erneuerbaren Energien«. In: Kriege um Ressourcen – Herausforderungen für das 21. Jahrhundert. Hg. Reiner Braun, Thomas Held, Eberhard Neugebohrn und Ole von Uexküll, München: Oekom.

World Wide Fund for Nature (2010). *Living Planet Report 2010. Biodiversität, Biokapazität und Entwicklung.* Berlin: WWF Deutschland.

Worldwatch Institute, Hg. (2010). *Zur Lage der Welt 2010. Einfach besser leben. Nachhaltigkeit als neuer Lebensstil.* München: Oekom.

Internet

de.wikipedia.org/wiki/Wachstumsrücknahme
www.degrowth.de
www.donnerwetter.de
www.europarl.de/de/europa_und_sie/das_ep/gesetzgebungverfahren.html
www.iwr.de
www.klimafakten.de
www.klimanavigator.de
www.klimaretter.info
www.noble-house.tk/de
www.pik-potsdam.de/~stefan/index.html (Homepage of Stefan Rahmstorf)
www.regenwald.org

About the author Werner Mittelstaedt

Werner Mittelstaedt has been active as an author, critical futurologist and future philosopher since the 1970s. He was the initiator and chairman of the Gesellschaft für Zukunftsmodelle und Systemkritik e.V. (GZS), which was founded in March 1977 and dissolved in August 2007. The GZS was active in the field of critical futures research and helped shape the German futures research scene. He is also the founder and editor of the journal BLICKPUNKT ZUKUNFT, which has been published since 1981 and is one of the oldest journals in the German-speaking world with a thematic focus on futures research and design. He is a founding member of the Netzwerk Zukunftsforschung (Future Research Network), which was established in 2007. Furthermore, Werner Mittelstaedt is the author of eleven social science, philosophical and popular science books that deal with the crises and future issues of global society and in which approaches to solutions are presented. He has also published a novel about climate change and well over 200 publications in books, magazines and on the internet.

Website: www.werner-mittelstaedt.com

About the author Wolf Heidecker

Wolf Heidecker is a trained performing artist/director and business manager who spent half of his professional career in the German arts industry as Admin and PR-officer, Tour Manager, Artistic Director and Chief Executive Officer/General Manager with several German opera and theatre companies. In Australia he has been working with the Queensland Philharmonic Orchestra, managing the Flying Fruit Fly Circus and the Wyndham Cultural Centre before becoming an independent theatre producer and director. He is also a Behavioural & Communications Analyst (Dr/USA), expertise and experiences that contribute to his artistic work.

Since 2001 based in Melbourne he produced and/or directed original Australian plays primarily with political and social justice topics as well as relevant musicals, shown at La Mama, fortyfivedownstairs, Wyndham Arts Centre, FCAC (Footscray), Theatreworks, Butterfly Club, The Potato Shed, and many other local and Victorian venues on tour. With the play Black Box 149 in 2017 Wolf initiated the first production of a play by an Australian playwright (Rosemary Johns) translated into German at the prestigious State Theatre Nuremberg/Germany.

With the support of the Australian Government Department of Social Services his production company WHAM in May 2021 realized a national tour of Bernard Clancy's play about PTSD Foxholes of the Mind.

Website: wolfsperformingartsmanagement.com

Performance Rights:

Written inquiries to

- WHAM Productions, Wolf Heidecker, PO Box 493, Werribee Vic 3030, Australia / email: whamflow@gmail.com

- Werner Mittelstaedt, Ecksteins Hof 50, 45721 Haltern am See, Germany / email: werner.mittelstaedt-gzs@t-online.de